"This almost-forgotten n
writers of all time is rev.
too-rarely-seen side of Yiddish literature and Jewish life;
its rendering here, by one of Jewish literature's greatest
translators, provides a crackling energy befitting its
material. Don't start it too late in the evening; you won't be
able to put it down."

—JEREMY DAUBER, Columbia University professor and
author of *The Worlds of Sholem Aleichem*

"This rediscovered short novel by Sholom Aleichem is a
gem—a vivid representation of the underside of Jewish
life in Eastern Europe, funny, touching, and biting. Curt
Leviant has done a remarkable job with the English
translation, aptly catching the pungent colloquial character
of the Yiddish."

—ROBERT ALTER, emeritus professor of Hebrew and
comparative literature, University of California, Berkeley,
and *author of The Hebrew Bible: A Translation with
Commentary*

"Moshkele Ganev flies in the face of so much of what we
think of when we imagine Eastern European Jewish life.
Here, Sholom Aleichem brings us the broadest of visions
of that world, not merely by dramatizing the shady
characters on society's margins, but also by inviting us
into their emotional lives and uncovering the complicated
power structures that can turn them into heroes. For
any reader who cares about the Jewish past, this never-
before-translated gem will be a revelation—and a delight."

—DARA HORN, author of *Eternal Life: A Novel*

"More than a century after his death, Sholom Aleichem has a new (or rather a newly rediscovered) book out, and it was worth the wait. Thanks to Curt Leviant for rescuing this unusual love story from obscurity, translating it so beautifully, and, at long last, giving it the readership it deserves."

—AARON LANSKY, author of *Outwitting History: The Amazing Adventures of a Man Who Rescued a Million Yiddish Books*

# Moshkeleh the Thief

University of Nebraska Press
*Lincoln*

# Moshkeleh the Thief

*A Rediscovered Novel*

SHOLOM ALEICHEM

*Translated from the Yiddish*
*with an introduction by*
Curt Leviant

The Jewish Publication Society
*Philadelphia*

Library of Congress
Cataloging-in-Publication Data
Names: Sholem Aleichem, 1859–1916, author. |
Leviant, Curt, translator, writer of introduction.
Title: Moshkeleh the thief: a rediscovered
novel / Sholom Aleichem; translated from the
Yiddish with an introduction by Curt Leviant.
Other titles: Moshḳele ganev. English
Description: Philadelphia: The Jewish
Publication Society, [2021] | Translated from
the 1913 edition of Moshkeleh Ganev.
Identifiers: LCCN 2021007243
ISBN 9780827615151 (paperback; alk paper)
ISBN 9780827618763 (epub)
ISBN 9780827618770 (pdf)
Classification: LCC PJ5129.R2 M64513 2021 |
DDC 839/.133—dc23
LC record available at
https://lccn.loc.gov/2021007243

Set in Arno Pro.

FRONTISPIECE: Sholom Aleichem,
ca. 1910. Bridgeman Images.

This book is dedicated to
my great-granddaughter
Tova Malka
טובה מלכה
carrying on a legacy of first-born daughters

My first-born daughter Dalya
and Harry Chefitz
gave birth to their first-born daughter, Leora,
who, with Ezra Spero
gave birth to their first-born daughter,
Tova Malka

I hope that just like her mother, Leora,
and her grandmother, Dalya,
have done
Tova Malka will also read
Sholom Aleichem in Yiddish with me

# Contents

# Acknowledgments

My thanks to the Yiddish teachers, the late Mikhl Baran, and his wife, Millie, for helping me interpret rare Yiddish words in the text and to the staff of the Yiddish Book Center for providing me with photocopies of various editions of *Moshkeleh Ganev*.

I also wish to express my gratitude to the director of The Jewish Publication Society (JPS), Rabbi Barry Schwartz, for so enthusiastically accepting my proposal to consider this Sholom Aleichem novel for the JPS list; and to the managing editor, Joy Weinberg, for her perceptive, tireless, and meticulous editing of the manuscript.

And thanks, too, to the University of Nebraska Press for being a publishing partner in this volume.

This entire project owes its fruition to the encouragement and advice of my wife, Erika, who urged me to start translating *Moshkeleh Ganev*. And when I finished and pondered where to send it, Erika wisely said, "Why don't you try The Jewish Publication Society? After all, they published your anthology, *Masterpieces of Hebrew Literature*, and also your novel *The Man Who Thought He Was Messiah*." I listened. So did JPS. Thanks, Erika.

# Introduction

Sholom Aleichem (Sholom Rabinowitz's pen name) was born in 1859, in the small Ukrainian town of Pereyaslav, and received both a traditional Jewish and a secular Russian education. Besides his mother tongue, Yiddish, he was also fluent in Hebrew, Russian, and Ukrainian. He began publishing humorous stories and sketches in the 1880s and, by early in the twentieth century, had become the most widely read writer in the history of Yiddish literature.

Sholom Aleichem came to the USA in 1914 and spent the final two years of his life in New York. His funeral, in 1916 (reported on page 1 of the *New York Times*), was the largest the city had ever seen: 150,000 people paid their last respects to the man who had become a legend in his own lifetime.

By no means was Sholom Aleichem a naïve folk writer. On the contrary, he was a conscious artist who knew classical Jewish sources and contemporary Yiddish and Hebrew literature. He was also well-read in West European and Russian literature, and was especially influenced by Gogol, who taught him about the comic grotesque, and Chekhov, embracing the latter's mingling of pathos and laughter.

One of Sholom Aleichem's great innovations was introducing into high-level imaginative writing the playful and ironic humor of the Jews that had hitherto only been part of the oral folk heritage.

He learned from older Yiddish authors like Mendele Mokher Sforim (1835–1917), whom he called "The Zeyde [Grandfather] of Yiddish Literature." Above all, Sholom Aleichem utilized Jewish folklore and Yiddish folk speech, which in its diversity, inventiveness, and range may be compared to the multilayered richness of Elizabethan English.

There are those who cling to the idea that the shtetl in Russia's Pale of Settlement was one warm and happy place—a latter-day Paradise. That this is a myth should be obvious to anyone reading the works of Sholom Aleichem. Certainly, there were moments of warmth and joy, especially on the Sabbath and Jewish holidays, but there was also poverty, hunger, antisemitism, second-class citizenship, insecurity, and pogroms. Sholom Aleichem, then, is not a chronicler of a romanticized shtetl, but a thoroughgoing realist with an almost all-encompassing vision of Jewish life in Russian surroundings, a writer who portrays the uneasy relationship between the minority and majority cultures.

True to his credo that fiction should engage with "events that are realistic, possible and plausible," Sholom Aleichem's world also contains revolutionaries, cardsharps, informers, and rogues—even adulterers and white slavers are hinted at. In other words, his re-creation of Jewish civilization in late nineteenth- to early twentieth-century Russia depicts a complete human comedy whose members represent various segments of the moral spectrum.

Sholom Aleichem painted for us a society that was vibrant when he was alive, but which, one generation after his death, the Germans and their collaborators in other parts of Europe turned to ashes and smoke.

The breadth of critical assessment that a writer gets—and the languages into which one has been translated—may be considered a measure of one's stature. Besides English, Sholom Aleichem has been translated into more than twenty European languages and also into Turkish, Japanese, Chinese, and Indonesian. More than six thousand articles and books have been written about him in Yiddish, Hebrew, English, Russian, Polish, French, and other languages, an indication of how well his work resonates in all cultures.

Films of Sholom Aleichem's stories have been made in Russia, Poland, and the USA. One of the greatest Yiddish films, *Tevye*, based on the beloved dairyman, starring and directed by Maurice Schwartz, was made in the United States in 1939, on a farm in Long Island. A musical adaptation of the Tevye stories, *Fiddler on the Roof*, a long-running hit on Broadway, was translated into other languages and performed around the world. The most recent revival of *Fiddler*, a translation back into Yiddish, staged at the National Yiddish Theatre Folksbiene in New York, also became a popular success.

*Moshkeleh Ganev* (*Moshkeleh the Thief*) was first serialized in Yiddish in a Warsaw newspaper in 1903 and then issued in book form three times over the next few decades: in 1913 (Warsaw), 1927 (Kiev), and 1941 (Moscow).

Interestingly, the Kiev and Moscow versions appeared under the aegis of the Communist regime, and adhering to the Soviet edict, all the Hebrew words in Sholom Aleichem's text were "transliterated" into Yiddish orthography, making the Hebrew words almost unrecognizable. This was done, ostensibly, to make it easier for readers of Yiddish who did not know Hebrew to properly read the text. The 1941 edition—under Stalin's despotic and antisemitic rule, no less—does have a four-page glossary, citing and explaining all the Hebrew words and phrases in *Moshkeleh Ganev*. An inadvertent benefit of this policy of transliterating the Hebrew is that it shows us precisely how Yiddish speakers in Russia pronounced the Hebrew words.

Up to the time he wrote *Moshkeleh Ganev*, Sholom Aleichem had never devoted a full-length work to the Jewish underclass. Here he gives us life in the raw, showing that Jewish shtetl society had, like the encompassing Russian society, its reprobates and its underworld.

*Moshkeleh Ganev* has a riveting plot, an unusual love story, and a superb, keenly observed portrayal of a lower-class Jew and his social milieu. We see a slice of late nineteenth-century Russian Jewish life, replete with fully fleshed characters of the sort that had never before been seen in Yiddish belles lettres. Striking, too, is the novel's depiction of Jews interacting with non-Jews in the Russian Pale of Settlement, a first and groundbreaking theme in modern Yiddish literature.

Why is it, then, that the standard twenty-eight-volume edition of Sholom Aleichem's works, *Ale Verk* (*The Collected Works*), published after the author's death, contains a variety of genres—novels, plays, memoirs both personal and literary, and hundreds of stories—but not this novel? We still do not know. As such, this novel may be considered a "lost," "rediscovered," "forgotten," or "neglected" work—or a combination of all four. Indeed, as of this writing, the following brief article and two citations, all of them in Yiddish, are the only items published regarding *Moshkeleh Ganev*:

- Avrohom Novershtern's "Vegn di publikatsye fun *Moshkeleh Ganev*" (Concerning the publication of *Moshkeleh Ganev*), published in 1984 in the premiere Yiddish arts and culture journal *Di Goldene Keyt* (The Golden Chain), is mostly devoted to the additions Sholom Aleichem made to *Moshkeleh* in reaction to the notorious April 1903 Kishinev pogrom—embellishments he later withdrew, realizing they had been made in the heat of emotion and pain and as such did not suit the novel's structure and esthetic fabric. Although the article by Hebrew University professor of Yiddish literature Novershtern does not specifically mention it, my hunch is that Sholom Aleichem wanted to add some elements re the Kishinev pogrom to the first printed volume, Warsaw 1913, but, as we know, he did not.[1]

- Two letters dated 1903 in *Dos Sholom Aleichem Bukh* (The Sholom Aleichem Book), an edited volume of letters by Sholom Aleichem published in 1926, note that he has completed the work and is proud of his accomplishment.[2]
- *Lexikon fun der Nayer Yiddisher Literatur* (Lexicon of Modern Yiddish Literature), volume 8, a long survey of the Yiddish writer's works published in 1981, simply states that Sholom Aleichem wrote *Moshkeleh Ganev* in 1903 and serialized it that same year.[3]

These sparse resources, however, are sufficient to attest to Sholom Aleichem's own view that *Moshkeleh Ganev* was an important literary achievement. In one of the two 1903 letters, he predicts that *Moshkeleh Ganev* will have the same success as his popular second novel, *Stempenyu* (1889). In the other he states: "I now feel as if I've been born anew, with new—brand new—strength. I can almost say that *now I've really begun to write.* [Sholom Aleichem's emphasis.] Until now I've only been fooling around."

*Moshkeleh Ganev* is also significant for Sholom Aleichem's approach to his material. Yiddish literature had long maintained a tradition of *edelkeyt*, refinement. Yiddish and Hebrew authors eschewed violence, the darker side of life, and people on the fringe of respectability. But *Moshkeleh Ganev* signals Sholom Aleichem's literary thrust away from this almost self-imposed silence. He writes with compassion, fidelity, and occasional humor about Jews from the underclass, thieves and petty criminals who challenge the mores of Jewish and general society. His main subject, in fact, is such a man: Moshkeleh, a horse thief rejected by society. Sholom Aleichem delves into their mores and foibles, their hopes and fears, even their thieves' argot—the first time that such piquant lingo, full of fascinating expressions, has been recorded in Yiddish literature. Indeed, in creating the character of Moshkeleh, Sholom Aleichem absorbed Chekhov's dictum: "To describe horse thieves in 700 lines I must all the time speak and think in their tone and feel in their spirit."

Perhaps most significant for literature in general is how *Moshkeleh Ganev* enriches our understanding of how these Jews, a minority culture, lived in Russia and interacted with non-Jews and melded into the broader Russian society. This novel lets us view the characters in the context of the majority culture, a Russian sociogeography as important and diverse as Chekhov's or Gogol's. Reading *Moshkeleh Ganev*, we feel as if previously unknown photographs of Russian life have suddenly been unearthed. Sholom Aleichem thus expands our understanding of East European Jewish and non-Jewish society, and offers us a glimpse of a segment of a population that existed but, by a conspiracy of silence, literary convention, or shame, was kept behind closed shutters in literature. By remaining true to his early esthetic of portraying unromanticized reality, Sholom Aleichem throws open these shutters for us.

In short, in this novel he enters a Jewish arena that had not hitherto been explored in Yiddish fiction. Perhaps this is why Sholom Aleichem himself felt that he had "been born anew."

And, we can only speculate, his exploration of then-controversial material may be why *Moshkeleh Ganev* was omitted from Sholom Aleichem's *Collected Works*. Perhaps conservative editors and even members of the author's own family—disregarding Sholom Aleichem's own high regard for the novel he himself considered transformative for his creativity—thought this book too radical in nature and not representative of the spirit of Sholom Aleichem, the humorist.

Regardless, by eclipsing the *edelkeyt* barrier in this 1903 novel, Sholom Aleichem paved the way for a more inclusive, more realistic, and less sentimental approach to describing the Jews in Eastern Europe. He inspired writers of succeeding decades to take up similar themes and, indeed, write about everything. Thanks to Sholom Aleichem, the next generation of Yiddish writers had no qualms representing the seamy side of Jewish life. Novelists and short story writers like Sholem Asch (1880–1957) and Nobel Laureate Isaac Bashevis Singer (1904–91), as well as other less well-known writers, broadened the range of Yiddish fiction by introducing Jewish smugglers, roughnecks, pimps, and prostitutes.

Serialized fiction was quite popular in Yiddish. Well into the middle of the twentieth century, Yiddish writers wrote novels in weekly installments for Yiddish newspapers with wide circulations, for instance, Isaac Bashevis Singer in the *Forward* and Chaim Grade in the *Day-Morning Journal*.

Since *Moshkeleh Ganev* was first serialized in a Warsaw Yiddish paper in 1903 in weekly installments, its structure is slightly different from a work intended for immediate publication as a book. An astute reader will note the rise and fall of action and the cliffhangers ending most chapters—compelling 1903 readers who wanted to know what came next to eagerly rush out and buy the next edition of the paper. Occasionally, Sholom Aleichem himself, like any to-be-continued author, calls attention to the suspense and tells his audience of fans to kindly read on.

The book's gripping story line and carefully honed Jewish and Christian protagonists make *Moshkeleh Ganev* unique and memorable. Crisp and tightly constructed, with an inventive and imaginative plot, Sholom Aleichem's novel has characters pulsing with life: the earthy tavern keeper, Chaim, and his starry-eyed daughter, Tsireleh; Moshkeleh, a kind of rudely shaped Tevye, a robust hero who lives beyond the border of respectability but is several notches down on the social ladder; and Maxim Tchubinski, Sholom Aleichem's objective depiction of a gentile who falls in love with Tsireleh—one of the rare non-Jewish characters in the writer's fiction.

With this debut publication of *Moshkeleh Ganev* in any language besides Yiddish and, obviously, the first translation into English, this innovative and influential novel has been restored to its rightful place among the Yiddish master's world-famous works.

## NOTES

1. Avrohom Novershtern, "Vegn di publikatsye fun *Moshkeleh Ganev*," *Di Goldene Keyt* 113 (1984): 34–41.
2. Y. D. Berkowitz, ed., *Dos Sholom Aleichem Bukh* (New York: Farlag Ikuf, 1926), 198–99.
3. Khone Shmeruk, ed., *Lexikon fun der Nayer Yiddisher Literatur*, vol. 8 (New York: Congress for Jewish Culture, 1981), column 678.

# Moshkeleh the Thief

CHAPTER 1

# Discusses Thieves

Non-Jews called him Moshke. Jews stretched out his name to "Moshkeleh" and then added the nickname *ganev*, or "thief"—for that's what he was, a ganev. Which means, he earned his livelihood by thievery.

But when it came to stealing, the only thing he stole was horses. In thieves' lingo, one doesn't say "I stole a horse." Rather, when speaking of their work, horse thieves say, "I shot a bird," or "I freed it from the stable . . ." or "whistled it out of the shed," or "I fiddled it out of a gypsy," or "whipped it out of a waggoner." . . . That's the jargon of horse thieves.

In fact, the word "ganev" wasn't even part of their vocabulary. A pickpocket was called "nimble fingers." One who worked in the dark was "a fly by night." A thief who stole from folks fast asleep at home was "an undercover man." A ganev of garments—"a coat collector." And a plain, run-of-the-mill robber was "a snatcher."

Moreover, the words "horse thief" were never articulated either. However, someone who had a great love, or amour, for horses—a man like that was called an "amateur."

And Moshkeleh Ganev was a great lover of horses. He adored horseflesh. Since childhood his daily fare had been riding a horse, flying like arrow from bow, jumping madly over hill and dale, into forests and across streams. His acquaintance with horses came via his father, Yoineh the Prophet, a life long horse thief.

Sorry! Not a thief, but a "prophet."

You know what a prophet is? Among horse thieves, horse dealers, and coachmen, a prophet is a know-it-all, a man who always gets it right. And at getting it right Yoineh the Prophet was an expert. Once, when two horses were taken from a coachman's stable, the coachman went straight to the Prophet.

"Reb Yoineh, what's to be done? I'm in a bad fix. Last night someone sneaked in and took off with two of my nags. Tell me what to do, Reb Yoineh!"

The Prophet Yoineh, elderly, gray, and cross-eyed—one eye looked south, the other north—was a man of few words.

"Which ones?" he asked.

"One was light bay; the other, dappled white. I just bought them at the fair. Traded my two mares for em. You know em, Reb Yoineh, they were good mares. I don't know what crazy notion got into me to trade em. Azriel, he should drop dead, started working on me, telling me, Swap em. Swap em. What's it to you if you swap em? So I went and swapped. And now this misfortune hit me. Help me! What should I do, Reb Yoineh?"

The Prophet looked to the side; his crossed eyes were blazing.

"Gimme a red one for the work."

"A red? Ten rubles? Where will I get such a big note? Things are rough, Reb Yoineh. Bitter, in fact. How about a green? Won't three rubles do, Reb Yoineh?"

The Prophet was still looking askance, his crossed eyes blazing. "Red."

"How about a blue, Reb Yoineh? Five rubles?"

"Red."

The coachman scratched himself, promised the Prophet ten rubles, returned home, and went to sleep. The next morning he woke up very early and found his two horses in the stable.

To make a long story short, Moshkeleh Ganev was a ganev and son of a ganev.

# CHAPTER 2

# He Displays His Mettle Early On

As a child Moshkeleh studied in the cheder. The Prophet, even though he himself was—and mum's the word—a ganev too, he still wanted his son to have a good Jewish education. Yoineh bragged to everyone that he was paying tuition for his "Kaddish"—the boy who would say the Mourner's Prayer for him when he died.

But the Kaddish preferred the stable to the school, and felt that a horse, forgive the comparison, was worth ten times more than the teacher. The teacher himself thought he had to report this to the father, albeit indirectly.

"Reb Yoineh, by the time your son gets to know the Kaddish, you'll already be dead."

These words struck the father so deep in his gut he went and got a hunting whip with leather thongs.

"Lie down!" he told Moshke. "You're gonna get your punishment."

But the son, with no great desire for a taste of the hunting whip on his naked flesh, refused the invitation. Under no circumstances would he lie down.

"Lie down!" said his father.

"I'm not lyin down," the son replied.

Yoineh's tone became sharper. "Lie down, I'm tellin you!"

"And I'm tellin you I'm not lyin down."

The father went berserk and tried to force Moshke down. But his son couldn't be budged. Yoineh struggled with him for an hour and got nowhere. He realized he could sooner lift his house than subdue his son.

"So you're not lyin down?" the father asked one last time.

"Nope. No way," the son answered. And to show his father he wasn't fooling around, Moshke pulled an iron horseshoe from his pocket and snapped it in two, like one breaks a bagel.

Seeing this, the Prophet realized that his son had Samson's strength and regarded him with great awe.

When Moshke left school, he didn't even know how to pray. As they would say in Mazepevke, "He's a bit slow with the Hebrew letters." Nevertheless, he knew other things: he could harness the biggest wagon and ride a horse like a Cossack. No matter how wild and fiery the horse, with Moshke on its back it became pliable like dough and quiet as a pussycat. And he also took like a duck to water; for him swimming back and forth from one side of the river to the other with one breath was a cinch.

His feats of strength were famous not only in Mazepevke but in all the surrounding villages. It was known that Moshke could wrestle three soldiers and single-handedly beat and pummel six men so badly blood would run. In brief, he wasn't easily forgotten.

Even at the tender age of thirteen, Moshke made his mark a few times, showing what he could do with his fists. The Mazepevke peasant lads, who almost every Sabbath picked fights with the Jewish boys as they took their Sabbath strolls along the streets, would sic their dogs on them, chase them, hoot at them, call them "Yids," and taunt them with antisemitic ditties.

But once they got the taste of Moshke's fists they spread the word not to start up with that Jew. And later, when Moshke grew and became a young man, the adult peasants too felt Moshke's paws and were scared to death of him.

One can say that getting into fights was a kind of wild passion for Moshke, an irresistible impulse, and he loved starting up with someone bigger and stronger than him.

Most often Moshke would display his brawn when someone was insulted. He'd thank God for his good luck at meeting some coachmen or butchers ganging up on one guy (it's well known that Jewish coachmen and butchers are a bunch of brutes). Seeing this, our Moshke would roll up his sleeves, jump right into the fire, and begin using his hands and feet, and, if necessary, butt with his head too.

More than one person would depart this fray with a lump on his forehead, black eyes and a bruised nose, and torn-off sleeves, ripped trousers, and rent jacket seams, as well.

At times Moshke himself also got a taste of this. And if somebody did lace into him—well, what can you do? In fact, Moshke liked a man who could dish it out. A guy like that, he would say, is someone worth smacking and a pleasure getting smacks from.

In short, when it came to blows, clouts, and punches, he had achieved renown. And I'll even say that at fisticuffs Moshke was a genius.

# CHAPTER 3

# His Fight with the Goliath of Zlodeyevke

Near Mazepevke, in the village of Zlodeyevke, lived a peasant named Ivan Kurka, tall and robust, a latter-day Goliath the Philistine. He was a decent, even placid chap—as long as he was sober. But when he had one drop too many, a murderous rage would take hold of him and he began to go wild, breaking down doors, smashing windows, and beating people, mostly Jews. At such times he would lash out against Jews in a life-threatening way.

"The Yids," he would complain, "embitter my life. They eat my flesh and drink my blood. I won't calm down until I kill every last one of them, one by one."

That's what Ivan Kurka would mutter to himself, until he got so drunk he finally had to be bound hand and foot like a ram and brought back to Zlodeyevke.

One day, Ivan Kurka brought two young oxen to market. Having sold them, he made his way to Sarah Voltziken's tavern, where he ordered one whiskey from her, a second, and yet a third—after which he turned furious. He unleashed his wild frenzy, as he usually did, breaking bottles and smashing windows, and then turned to harassing Sarah Voltziken, first with words, then curses, and finally with slaps and blows.

People started yelling:

"Sarah Voltziken's being beaten!"

The outcry was so loud it reached the market, where Moshke, wearing his short fur jacket, trousers tucked into his boots, and whip in hand, stood among the horse dealers, looking over a horse he had his heart set on.

Suddenly he heard the shout:

"Sarah Voltziken's being beaten!"

"By who?"

"Ivan Kurka."

Swifter than an eagle, fleeter than a deer, stronger than a leopard, Moshke raced into Sarah Voltziken's tavern and with just one furious smash of his fist into Ivan Kurka's face, he made blood run from his left ear.

A few days later Ivan Kurka came to Mazepevke. He ambled about town, his cheek swollen, carrying a big pot of eggs and asking:

"Where does that Yid who beat me up live?"

Naturally, the Mazepevke Jews didn't want to reveal Moshke's address. But once Moshke got wind of who was looking for him, Moshke himself went up to Ivan Kurka and said:

"You lookin to get your puss clouted a coupla more times?"

To which Ivan Kurka replied:

"No, thanks, that one smack was enough for me. And to show you I mean what I say, look, I got you a present. Eggs."

And from then on, Ivan Kurka became Moshke's friend.

In fact, they became bosom pals.

# CHAPTER 4

# He Dislikes Mazepevke Jews, and Justifiably So

Thereafter, the Mazepevke Jews were able to sleep in peace.

Moshke, or as he was known in town, Moshkeleh Ganev, was their protector. Indeed, he was naught but a thief, ostracized by the community, the sort of person no man would seek as a match for his daughter. Nevertheless, when Moshke was needed, people would flatter and cajole him, try to creep into his good graces, and shower him with scores of compliments. As the Yiddish folk saying has it: "If you need the thief, you take him from the gallows."

None of this passed Moshke by and he laughed up his sleeves at them all. The Jews of Mazepevke, along with the richest man in town, weren't worth more to him, as he himself put it, "than a bent nail in an old horseshoe."

Nevertheless, Moshke bore them lots of resentment.

First of all, for the name itself. He knew that behind his back they called him Moshkeleh Ganev. How did they come up with calling him a thief? From which Jews in town had he, God forbid, stolen? And why was his name stretched out to Moshkeleh? Why did he deserve to be called Moshkeleh Ganev, when Moishe Naftoles the money lender was the real ganev and a usurer, the sort about whom every nasty thing was said? Yet, that money lender the local Jews called Moisheleh, and he was even given the honorific

Reb Moisheleh. Why? Because Moishe Naftoles had money and Moshke did not.

He also resented that when he came to shul on a holiday, he had no place to sit but was obliged to stand somewhere behind the bimah.

He resented too that on Simkhas Torah, the holiday when Jews danced with Torahs around the bimah for the Seven Circuits, he was either given a Torah only for the very last circuit, a tiny Torah with a torn coverlet, or he wasn't even given a Torah at all.

He also resented that he'd never had the honor of being invited to a celebration, a bris or a wedding, even though he had never quarreled with anyone or taken anything from anyone, God forbid, nor had he ever insulted or badmouthed anyone.

In fact, he was on good terms with everyone. And when it came to doing a favor for a fellow Jew, lending someone a hand in the middle of the night—he did that wholeheartedly. Not to mention helping a poor man out with a ruble, because for Moshke a ruble had no value at all. . . .

"Rubles," he would say, "God has plenty of them, and money is round. Today the other guy has it, tomorrow it's mine."

But above all Moshkeleh resented that no one wanted to make a match with him. No one wanted him. No girl, not even a housemaid of the lowest rung, wanted to marry him. Better a tailor or a shoemaker for a husband, she would say—anyone but Moshkeleh Ganev.

Moshke had heard these very words with his own ears from a poor, barefoot girl called Leya, who didn't even have a stitch of clothes to her name. Admittedly, it wasn't very pleasant hearing such remarks. But, despite all this, Moshkeleh Ganev did marry, and what's more, he took a pretty girl, the prettiest one in town.

She even came from a genteel and well-to-do family. And what a family it was!

About this event a saying was created in Mazepevke—the worst dog gets the best bite.

And they were absolutely right.

# CHAPTER 5

# Chaim Chosid's Daughter Scandalizes Mazepevke and the Town Goes Topsy-Turvy

The most notable worthies in Mazepevke come to drink wine at Chaim Chosid's wine cellar: town officials, priests, and just plain householders—because first of all, Chaim Chosid had the best wines, and, secondly, the ambience was very pleasant.

Chaim Chosid himself was not much to look at, but to make up for that he had a singularly attractive wife whom the higher-ups in town called Chaimova, and daughters, one lovelier than the other.

Chaimova and her girls were well-known in Mazepevke and—you know what?—drinking a fresh glass of wine just drawn from the barrel was quite delicious when a beautiful woman served you and pretty girls were always in sight. You might say, what's the fuss? That doesn't make the wine any sweeter. Still, it was much more enjoyable with the girls around.

Chaim Chosid was well aware of this. The town bigshots themselves often told him that he had a beautiful wife and good-looking daughters. But he disregarded these remarks. Because he knew his wife and daughters very well, he slept soundly at night and felt tranquil and secure.

But Mazepevke is a town where people love to prattle. If Jews start blabbing about you, may God Himself come and help. Nevertheless, no one dared unleash his tongue against Chaim Chosid's wife and daughters. If anyone did want to make a comment, he only said:

"A pretty wife and good-looking daughters is the best good luck charm for making a living."

And did not add another word.

After this introduction, it's easy to picture the reaction in town when Chaim Chosid's daughter, the beautiful Tsireleh, the youngest, quietest, and most accomplished of his daughters, ran away from home after the first Pesach Seder. And with whom did she flee? With one of the Christian burghers, the town liquor tax collector named Maxim Tchubinski. And where did they run off to? To the monastery. Did you hear that? Right to the monastery itself.

Where can one find a pen to depict all the happenings that Pesach in Mazepevke? Where can one get the colors to paint the scene . . . how the stricken Chaim Chosid lay with his face pressed to the ground, and the entire household, the children, and even the maids, their faces on their pillows, crying more than the most pious Jews weep nowadays on the Ninth Day of Av, mourning the destruction of the Holy Temple in Jerusalem.

After the Seder everyone in Mazepevke was on the move. From indoors to outside of the house, Monastery Street was inundated with men and women, boys and girls. One can't even begin to record the stories that made the rounds and the rumors that flew that night, the next day, and throughout all the days of Pesach.

CHAPTER 6

# Chaim Chosid's Son-in-Law Has an Idea

In the heat of the moment, Chaim Chosid could do nothing. So, not knowing what to do, he locked himself into his room, rolled about on the floor, and wept. The tears he shed were worse, a thousand times worse, than weeping for the dead, because for the latter it is solely grief. But here grief was fused with humiliation.

Chaim's wife acted differently. Chaimova ran off to the most prominent Christian burghers. She cast herself at the feet of the town council chief himself, crying and pleading for compassion, as she requested permission to see her daughter, if only for half an hour. But weeping was of no avail.

They could only help her with sweet words.

"Your daughter will in no way be harmed, God forbid," were their consoling words. "With God's help she will be happy, because Maxim Tchubinski is a very upstanding and honest man. She'll surely have a much better life with him than with any Itzko or Berko you and your husband will choose for her."

That's how these good people consoled the poor mother's embittered heart. But the poor mother did not want to be consoled. From the head of the town council she ran to the priests, to the monks of the monastery, prostrating herself, kissing their feet—but no cry to God could help.

Then one of Chaim Chosid's sons-in-law came up with an idea:

"Moshkeleh Ganev! What I mean is, let's turn to Moshkeleh Ganev. He'll find a way.... He knows how to do it. For him you don't have to spell it out."

When one is drowning one grabs hold of a sword's blade. So Chaim Chosid sent someone to bring a message to Moshkeleh Ganev:

"Please come to our house to discuss a very urgent matter with us."

Moshke had just returned home from "work" with his hot, sweaty horse. Nevertheless, without even dusting himself off, he departed, grimy, hungry and thirsty, to Reb Chaim Chosid to hear about this "very urgent matter," although deep down he sensed it was about Chaim Chosid's runaway daughter, Tsireleh.

At once Moshke's heart began pounding and he didn't know why.

It wasn't easy for Chaim Chosid and his family to initiate this discussion with Moshkeleh Ganev. Nor was it easy for Moshkeleh Ganev to ask why he had been summoned. Both parties sat absolutely mute for a long, long time.

Finally, someone broke the silence: Eli Noah, the oldest son-in-law, a well-spoken young man and Bible scholar, who wore a silk cap even in mid-week, presented himself as an advocate for the entire family, choosing his words very carefully, like someone slowly eating matza.

"What happened, you see, is that our Tsireleh, my young sister-in-law, what she did was ... you see, she went off, that is to say, not alone, I mean, yes, alone, but not, you know, not by herself, to the other side, to the, so to speak, enemy camp, and so, from there, you see, she has to be, you get what I'm driving at, so we've decided that ... if you want to, that is to say, if you agree, you can make a ruble...."

Here Eli Noah stopped, craned his neck like someone with a bone stuck in his throat, and wanted to continue talking.

But Moshke Ganev interrupted him, mimicking Eli Noah's halting manner of speech:

"The long and short of this, you see, is that you're a full-fledged jerk, you see, but you think, if you get my drift, you're as smart as all get-out. Folks say, you know, that a ram has a long horn, but it still can't, that is to say, it still can't blow its own shofar. As I live and breathe, the ruble you're offerin me, I swear I'm gonna donate in honor of your uncle's yortzeit, and may my name no longer be Moshke if I don't take Tsireleh out of the monastery, even if I die tryin."

These words of Moshke's were said so resolutely and with such heartfelt emotion that everyone listening was dumbstruck with amazement. And even Eli Noah, who was perspiring and had turned red with humiliation, was pleased. He looked from side to side, sniffed, and licked his lips like a cat about to get a taste of the Pesach goosefat.

Tsireleh's mother, Chaimova, who had been weeping all along now, stopped crying and, wringing her hands, said:

"Amen! From your mouth to God's ears. That's my wish, dear God, Master of the Universe."

But Chaim Chosid sat with his head lowered, gazing down at the floor. He just couldn't look anyone in the eye, as though all this was his fault, and he was guilty of some deed too shameful to even speak of.

And when Moshkeleh Ganev stood to say good-bye and leave, Chaim Chosid looked at Moshke with such despair and with so much hope that anyone else besides Moshke would have just melted with compassion for Chaim Chosid.

Instead, Moshkeleh Ganev went up to Reb Chaim Chosid cheerfully, put his hands on his shoulders and, as though speaking to one's lifelong pal, said most amicably:

"Don't you worry none. Everything's gonna be all right."

Moshkeleh Ganev's approaching him and placing his hands on his shoulders, along with his "Don't you worry none," was enough of a comedown for Chaim Chosid, who had never before even met Moshke Ganev and had never heard him speak. But if God wants to punish someone, He metes it out in all directions.

And, recalling the biblical Job and his endless suffering, Chaim Chosid let out a deep sigh and, using the popular Hebrew/Yiddish saying, uttered:

"This too is for the good."

# CHAPTER 7

# Turns Back for a While to Discuss Lofty Matters

If tall stature, broad shoulders, sturdy legs, and a big head of curly black hair makes one handsome, then one can say that our hero was a handsome young man. If not for the fact that he was Moshkeleh Ganev, he could have found many girls in Mazepevke willing to have him and, besides, offer a dowry too.

Word had it in town that some Mazepevke girls liked him a lot and some actually even longed for him, burying this secret deep in their hearts and perhaps even carrying it with them to the grave.

Moshkeleh Ganev would often meet Chaim Chosid's daughters during the Sabbath afternoon strolls, looking them over carefully and, as the saying goes, devouring them with his eyes. But Chaim Chosid's daughters were as far removed from him as Moshke was from them, and he even feared thinking of them for more than a moment, although they appealed to him very much—especially the youngest one, Tsireleh.

He had once met Tsireleh in a narrow lane and almost stopped and kissed her. Luckily, Henekh the slaughterer, with earlocks rounded like thin little bottles, was just passing by and fixed his calf-like eyes on the two of them, just gazing, as if he didn't care a whit about them.

Moshke met Tsireleh again when he was riding his horse and noticed her and her sisters on their way to bathe in the stream.

Seeing him on the horse, Chaim Chosid's daughters stopped to watch Moshkeleh Ganev riding. Aware of the girls' glances, he spurred his horse and galloped like a whirlwind to the river. Then he turned right back, for he yearned to start talking with them but didn't have the nerve to begin before they spoke first.

They too wanted to have a word with him, but how would it look for Chaim Chosid's daughters to speak openly to a man, especially the likes of Moshkeleh Ganev? Still, he pranced about in front of the girls, accompanying them right up to the water. He trotted back and forth for a while until it dawned on him that they could not undress because of him, and so he galloped away to the outskirts of town and disappeared.

There were many other such encounters, all of them without any exchange of words, and it never dawned on Tsireleh to ask:

What's going on? Why does Moshke keep coming by so often?

Like Chaim Chosid's other daughters, Tsireleh had already become accustomed to having men look at her. In her father's wine cellar she had grown used to hearing compliments and experiencing even worse: for instance, a stroke on the arm, a pinch on the cheek, and the like, which the lowlifes there permitted themselves.

But this isn't the way it happened with our hero, Moshke.

Not for a minute did Moshke cease thinking of Tsireleh. Her entire presence, her beautiful, sunny face with its short nose, little double chin, and white throat, and her gray, somewhat stern eyes always stood in the forefront of his thoughts by day and in his dreams at night.

As he galloped way behind town on his fiery horse, like arrow from bow, he would often shout out Tsireleh's name. To the broad expanse of quiet meadow he revealed his sacred secret, telling the trees of the green forest about his love for Chaim Chosid's daughter, and sharing his concerns with the little crystal stream flowing behind the woods:

What should I do? What should I do?

But not the broad expanse of quiet meadow, not the green forest, and not the crystal stream could provide an answer or offer Moshke advice. And so he urged his horse on and sped off to cast away his secret thoughts and buried emotions into the far distance.

If among the Mazepevke Jews one could find someone truly in love, with a love that was pure, holy, and sincere, one without any hidden motives, and without any hope—it was Moshkeleh Ganev.

# CHAPTER 8

# Which Strays Off Course a Bit, Yet Still Has Relevance to the Novel

Since we have already spoken of lofty matters like love, we must also note that our hero, Moshkeleh Ganev, had already once had a taste of romance but, alas, it did not go his way.

It occurred when he was quite young and had begun to accompany his father, the Prophet Yoineh, to the fairs.

Now, for his first time at the Yarmeniletz Fair, Moshke went with his father to the inn where all the horse traders, horse merchants, horse thieves, and just plain ganevs stayed, most of them Jews with strange red faces and fiery eyes. They were a vivacious bunch, shrewd and experienced, who understood one another with just a wink.

Growing up among thieves, it was nothing new for our hero to meet such folk, who spoke their own lingo, constantly looked about suspiciously, and lived in constant fear, always on alert that the police were on their way to nab and jail them.

But the ganevs Moshke encountered for the first time at the Yarmeniletz Fair were a totally new breed. Pure flame and fire, they were demons in human guise. Compared to these chaps, the Mazepevke thieves were kids, dunderheads. What he witnessed in Yarmeniletz he had never seen before; what he heard here he had never heard before.

Moshke scrutinized these men carefully, paid close attention to their manner of speech. This new experience gave him strange pleasure and brought him lots of joy.

Most of all he got to like the elder of the pickpockets. He was old, short, compact, with broad shoulders; a wide, wispy, gray beard; and starkly red-rimmed eyes that constantly flashed and blinked. His head, seemingly without any neck, grew right out of his broad shoulders, and when he had to look around, he had to turn his entire body.

Strange too were the elder's hands, which were unlike those of other people. They were long and wide, with oddly bent fingers. Yet, these hands and unusual fingers, at which Moshke gazed incessantly, were blessed hands and highly accomplished fingers, thanks to which he had earned great renown among the thieves.

Once these hands and fingers made their way toward a little pocket watch or a wallet filled with money, they would pluck the prize so quickly the victim, even if he had eighteen pairs of ears, would not have heard him doing his work. In his youth, this elder had already been in jail a few times with all the lock breakers and robbers. Finally, he got sick of that and joined a fraternity of pickpockets as an elder, offering them as a dowry of sorts the skills of his daughter, Sonke, who had inherited her father's blessed hands and highly accomplished fingers.

# CHAPTER 9

# An Undeserved Slap

At that time Sonke wasn't even quite fifteen, but she looked like a girl of eighteen, blooming like a young rose with its beautiful, fragrant, velvety petals. She gazed out at God's world, lively and full of joy, with faith and confidence: with faith that the world is good and sweet; with confidence that people are honest and nice.

Sonke was swarthy and charming, with curly black hair, black sizzling eyes, and dimples in her round cheeks. Her small white teeth were always seen, for she laughed a lot and this made others laugh too. With Sonke present there was no gloom. She had a liveliness in her, a joy that could drive away the deepest melancholy, like sunshine on an early summer morning, when the birds get together to sing Psalms.

But regarding Sonke, Moshke felt that something wasn't quite right. He sensed she was like a bone in his throat. Not that he couldn't stand her, God forbid. On the contrary. All day long, while she was out working, he missed her terribly, as though she were close kin, a sister.

But when she returned from work, changed her clothes, and sat down to eat and drink with all the other pickpockets, and, as usual, begin laughing—this pierced Moshke in the gut. Above all he was angry with her for being attached to a one-eyed, pockmarked young chap, who nevertheless was a superb night ganev, specializing in robbing folks who were fast asleep. Sonke would continually whisper to him and go out with him to ply her trade.

This Moshke couldn't stand. He had plans to discuss this with her a number of times and to rebuke her, but it never came about. Until one day he met Sonke as she was on her way to the market, all alone, dressed in men's clothing.

Moshke stopped her.

"Wait a second," he said. "I wanna tell you something."

"Who are you?"

"Don't you recognize me? Moshke from Mazepevke, the Prophet Yoineh's son."

"So what's it you wanna say, Prophet's son from Mazepevke?"

"What kind of buddy-buddy is that pockmarked night ganev to you?"

"What's it to you, you dumb jackass?"

"All I gotta do is whistle once and you'll get a taste of what kind of dumb jackass I am."

And before our Moshke could blink, he got such a sharp, resounding, stinging slap in the face from Sonke's hand with its very accomplished fingers that he was stunned, not so much from the blow itself as the humiliation, that he, Moshke, should be slapped by a girl!

The slap in itself wouldn't have been so bad had no one known about it. But worst of all was that when she came home from work, Sonke herself boomed out the news at the inn, trumpeting it to the whole crowd while laughing heartily and showing everyone her white teeth.

Moshke, glad that the fair was over, returned home with his father, carrying in his heart the image of Sonke's little hand with its accomplished fingers. This image, which he could not forget for a long time and even manifested itself in his dreams, reminded him of that sharp, resounding, stinging slap and that sharp, resounding, stinging little laugh of hers.

But since all this had happened so long ago, the wound from the slap had healed and the romance was long forgotten.

# CHAPTER 10

# Moshke Has a Plan

Even on his way to Chaim Chosid's house Moshke had already come up with a plan. And not only one but several at once.

One was to dress up as a monk; another was to disguise himself as a beggar; yet another was to go to the monastery, pass himself off as a functionary of the excise tax office, lead the Jewish girl out, carry her off on his horse, and flee with her to the end of the world.

But once he had thoroughly considered all these plans, he realized how foolish they were and rejected them all. Then he came up with an entirely new plan, one that was at once dangerous and grand.

Moshkeleh entered the monastery, went straight to the head monk, and poured out to him his embittered heart:

"Since I'm considered an outcast among the Jews, no one wants to have anything to do with me. No one wants to arrange a marriage with me, and everybody calls me a very insulting name: ganev, or thief. So that's why I wanna repent. I wanna change my line of work, my name, even my religion. But since I'm scared the Jews are gonna plague me, I'm asking you in the monastery to protect me from the hands of the Jews."

The monastery elder heard him out, questioned him at length, welcomed him, and gave him a room.

"No harm, God forbid, will befall you," the elder assured him, and this sufficed for Moshke.

But he did want Tsireleh to take interest in him, the newcomer to the monastery, and to get to know him.

Moshke's reckoning, in fact, was right on the mark.


Tsireleh sat all by herself, as though in prison. No one was allowed to see her. But having heard that a young man from Mazepevke had entered the monastery to take on the new faith, she was very eager to know, first of all, who was this Jew. She also wanted some news from home, about her family, for whom her heart had not ceased to yearn. And how surprised Tsireleh was when she saw that the man standing before her was Moshkeleh Ganev.

Tsireleh knew him well, for who didn't know Moshkeleh Ganev in Mazepevke? But she couldn't fathom what had prompted him, a free bird who did as he pleased and pursued whatever his heart longed for, to come here to the monastery. And she wasn't ashamed at all to ask him:

"What's the meaning of all this?"

Moshke poured out his embittered heart to Tsireleh and confessed in full:

"Since the Jews consider me an outcast, no one in Mazepevke wants to have anything to do with me," he said, using the very same words he had told the monastery elder, and he concluded with a sigh, saying, "Although it was very difficult for me to come here, I still feel life is so bitter, so bitter. . . ."

Tsireleh pitied him with all her heart; she consoled him and poured out all her troubles to Moshke:

"I too struggled with myself at great length until I finally decided to abandon my father and mother, my sisters and brothers. My heart is breaking for them and there's no way I can help them . . .

It's all over and done with," Tsireleh concluded. "Over and done with, because right after their holiday . . ."

With the words, "their holiday," Tsireleh caught herself and turned red as fire. Then she said goodbye to Moshke and added:

"Very likely we'll see each other again tomorrow in the monastery courtyard."

"Perhaps in the garden?" he asked.

"Perhaps in the garden," Tsireleh repeated.

# CHAPTER 11

# A Walk in the Monastery Garden

As far back as Moshke could remember, he had never before spent a night without a wink of sleep nor one beset by so many apprehensions. Moshke had already proven he could ride his horse ten miles without stopping; he had already shown he could run off with liberated horses, could ride while hearing bullets flying behind his back. He had also jumped over fences, swum across streams, withstood the greatest dangers.

But never in his life had he experienced a night like this at the monastery. He paced back and forth in his little alcove, like a lion in a cage, staring out the window, looking forward to the dawning of day. And, with the help of God, when morning came, Moshke told one of the monks that he was going to town for an hour or so to tend to his horses. And he indeed returned within an hour, out of breath, looking like a man who had done some strenuous tasks.

The monks at the monastery wondered why Moshke's hands were so scratched up as though he had just leaped over a fence. But he calmed them, saying it had to do with his horses, and then went to see the monastery elder pertaining to his repentance.

During the day, when the monks finish eating and take an afternoon nap or head out to do their work, and the entire monastery is still and not a soul is in sight—no strangers, no worshippers, no beggars—Tsireleh would go out into the courtyard for a while, walking from one side to another aimlessly, just going out for a stroll.

But now she looked to all sides, searching for someone, then spotted Moshke treading the ground with his big feet. She approached him with a friendly smile, which at once ignited a hellish fire in his heart. But, restraining himself with great effort, he sat down on a stump of a recently cut tree.

"Come," Tsireleh called out, "why should we sit here?"

"Then where should we go?"

"Let's walk around here," she said.

"How about the garden?" Moshkeleh asked.

Tsireleh stopped for a minute, pondered, then replied:

"The garden? All right, the garden."

The monastery garden in Mazepevke was akin to a fortress to which access from the outside was difficult. On one side, the one that faced town, stood a high, leaf-covered stone fence. On the other side was a ditch lined with thorns and thistles.

The garden itself was one of the great wonders, an earthly Paradise, as it was called in Mazepevke, even though no Jew had ever had the privilege of setting foot in it.

The only benefits the Jews derived from the garden were enjoying the scent of the trees brought by the summertime breezes and listening to the nightingales sing there during the warm summer nights.

Pesach time. Spring was just reawakening. The earth wasn't yet fully green. On the trees of the monastery garden, one could already see tiny yellow buds, from which any moment now—just let the sun warm them—little green leaves would appear. It was sheer joy to breathe in the fresh scent of the still damp earth, covered here and there with green velvet. Some birds flitted among the branches, hopping from one tree to another. There they stopped, pecked their beaks into the bark, blinked and chirped quietly, spreading the news that soon summer would be on its way.

Spring is the time when one yearns to be outdoors, even more than in the summer. Now sunshine is most welcome, each ray a gift of God. This is when man feels his link to the earth, to everything on it, to the entire world itself, and to his bond with the One who created this vast universe.

The two of them, both Moshke and Tsireleh, proceeded quietly, immersed in their own thoughts, overtaken by their own feelings. Both floated in that upper realm, in Paradise, whose name is Love.

This was the kind of love that brooked no restraints, that needed no commentary. The kind that sunders iron chains, shatters fortified walls, separates the near and unites those farthest away. It was the kind of love that can accomplish impossible deeds.

# CHAPTER 12

# Hens Lay Eggs, Jewish Girls Make Babies

Raised in a home like Chaim Chosid's, under the supervision of a pious father and a devoted mother, Tsireleh saw what sort of life her older sisters had made for themselves and the type of husbands given them, one a bigger fool than the other.

Tsireleh had always longed for a different life. Her attitude was unlike that of her sisters, whose routine consisted of getting pregnant, giving birth and rocking the cradle, and then going through that cycle again and yet again. Her sisters were busy day and night, without an hour to themselves, constantly obliged to remember the words of the Hebrew precept: "Do the will of your husband."

Quite often Tsireleh would mull over the destiny of a Jewish girl, which she compared to that of a clucking hen who sits on her eggs and warms them until the chicks peck their way out of their shells—whereupon that hen then begins clucking again, creates more eggs, and so on.

No offense meant by that comparison, but I have to tell you that Chaim Chosid's house was full of such cluckers. All his other daughters married at a young age, one after the other, to silken young men, neat little sons-in-law, all of whom, supported by father-in-law Chaim Chosid, kept producing children.

And also Chaim Chosid's wife, who was not yet old, kept getting pregnant and giving birth. At mealtime, then, several mothers always sat around the table nursing their babies, while from the cradles came the peep-peeping of tiny chicks.

One can say that hardly a month passed without some celebration, a mazel tov for a birth, a bris, a redemption ceremony for a first-born son; or, the reverse, one child with measles, another feverish with chicken pox, this one with diphtheria, that one with scarlet fever.

The mothers also had their problems, day and night: a difficult childbirth, a to-do with her breast, a wet nurse who quit in the midst of her breast-feeding, a nanny who almost crippled a child.

Perpetual tumult, commotion, pandemonium filled the house.

Into this hubbub entered Reb Sholom the matchmaker to arrange a prospective husband for the youngest daughter, Tsireleh. She listened to Reb Sholom's entire spiel as he proposed a respectable match, along the lines of his previous ones: a young man from a fine, reputable family.

And Tsireleh imagined that they had already chosen for her a husband akin to the ones her older sisters got, the likes of an Eli Noah, a chap who spoke well and knew the Bible and wore a silk cap in mid-week, and that she was already married to such a man and had begun to have children, and problems with her breast, the wet nurse, and the nannies.

Picturing this, Tsireleh became disgusted with the world, with life, and with people, and she promised herself that she would not marry the way her sisters had. She would build her life differently.

But how?

Exactly how Tsireleh herself did not know.

Just at this time she got to know the newly appointed town liquor tax collector, Maxim Tchubinski.

# CHAPTER 13

# On Philosophy, Love, and Other Matters

When the town's new liquor tax collector, Maxim Tchubinski, arrived in Mazepevke, he paid the customary visit to Chaimova in the wine cellar, where he tasted Chaim's "Vermouth." All the town's worthies were well aware it was made from raisins, but nevertheless they loved to drink it, and considered it "not bad at all," especially if that "Vermouth" was served by one of Chaimova's daughters, and, above all, by the youngest, Tsireleh, whom the worthies nicknamed "Mademoiselle Cecilia."

Whoever was served by "Mademoiselle Cecilia" felt privileged, for not everyone had the good fortune of getting that bit of wine from her.

And since Tchubinski was a new guest and the excise collector too, Chaimova saw to it that Tsireleh should not be shy and serve the guest in the proper fashion. Tsireleh was not shy and she did serve the guest in the proper fashion.

The wine cellar regulars sang the praises of "their Jewish girl" to the new tax collector, while exchanging clever and very pointed remarks, amid gales of odd laughter and bizarre winks.

Tchubinski was the only one in the group who did not laugh. From the very first moment he saw this beautiful Jewish girl he began reflecting, racking his brains: where had he seen her before?

Has it ever happened to you that on a journey you bump into someone you're sure you've already met before? Or hear a remark you've apparently already heard? But where and when—you can't possibly recall.

Learned folk express various conjectures and speculate that among human beings there exists a magnetic force that pulls one person to another, an energy that brings two people together from great distances even before they have ever met or heard about each other.

Philosophers have nothing better to do. They talk on and on until they finally conclude that something exists which we call "a match made in heaven."

Some match! Maxim Tchubinski and Chaim Chosid's daughter.

But let's cast philosophy aside and return to our novel.

Only one language in the world has no alphabet, no grammar, no vocabulary, no dictionary. This language, called "love," is spoken not by the mouth but by eyes alone. One meaningful glance sends a message. A squeeze of the hand suffices.

In this language our heroes conversed. And they evidently understood each other quickly, for hardly a month had passed from the day Maxim Tchubinski arrived in Mazepevke when he posted a letter to his only good friend, his mother, who lived in the far-off province of Saratov.

In this letter Tchubinski bared his heart and told his mother the whole story:

"I have met a Jewish girl whose image I've been carrying in my heart. And I fell so madly in love with her I was going out of my mind. After wrangling with the passion within me, and with Satan, I finally decided to disclose my feelings to the girl and reveal my secret to her—*I just can't live without you.*

"When she heard those words, the girl began to cry. 'Unfortunately,' she declared, 'nothing will come of this, for I come of Jewish stock.'

"So then I consoled her and said:

'I want to show you that in this world some matters are so supremely important that for them one leaves one's home, bids farewell to one's parents, and changes everything: one's home, one's name, and one's faith.'

"At this she began to weep in earnest. Nevertheless, she pressed close to me and begged me, 'At least give me a few more days to think it over.'"

Maxim Tchubinski offered other details to his mother; and, in keeping with his long-standing habit of telling her nothing but the truth, he did not conceal a thing.

To this letter Maxim received a short reply:

"If the girl you have chosen is worthy of the name Tchubinski—and I have no doubts about this, for I trust you, my son—and if your feelings toward the girl are indeed so resolute that you have no other choice, then I send you, my beloved son, my blessings and I wish you good fortune, and I hope that God will surely forgive you, for you will be saving a soul. . . ."

And so on and so forth—the usual words a mother writes to her son.

# CHAPTER 14

# Jews Buy Wine for the Seder

Throughout the year Chaim Chosid's wine cellar is open to the town worthies. But on the Eve of Pesach, Chaim and his entire family, including the wine cellar and all its wine, are held in bondage to the Children of Israel in Mazepevke.

To get a sense of what happened at the Exodus of the Jews from Egypt, please come down to Chaim Chosid's cellar when the Mazepevke Jews buy wine for the Four Cups of the Seder.

All year long Jews manage to survive, thank God, without wine. They make Kiddush over challah and drink water from the stream. But with Pesach coming they get spoiled and pampered. They prepare themselves to become kings at the Seder, as tradition prescribes. Now they think they're sophisticated connoisseurs and experts in wines.

At this season, plain wine is nothing but junk. For Pesach, people demand a Vermouth, and a fine one at that, from the best vineyards. But hold it! A plain Vermouth is junk too. It should also have a hint of Merlot. Still, that too is bilge water. For it should be blended with a wine that makes the tip of your tongue tingle and doesn't give you heartburn, and yet is strong and goes down smoothly.

"You know, Reb Chaim, you know what I want. The one I bought last year, remember?"

Such are the remarks Chaim Chosid hears the day before Pesach, and not just from one man. He hears this from ten, twenty, fifty of the town's Jews at the same time, for all of them postpone getting their Four Cups till the last possible day, the final hour, the very last minute.

And no matter how much Chaim scolds them for shopping so late, it helps like cupping helps a corpse. It just doesn't sink in.

"You're absolutely right," they say but continue to do exactly what they've done in the past.

On this day neither Chaimova nor her daughters work in the cellar alone. Chaim Chosid himself joins them, along with his sons-in-law. One pours wine, one washes bottles, one offers samples. A veritable racket encompasses the cellar: shouts, noise, tumult. One customer's order was mixed up—he got the wrong bottles of wine; that one didn't pay; another's bottle broke and he stands there, his fingers around the corked glass neck, asking:

"What should I do now?"

Another customer yells: "Give me two liters of the kind I got last year, and one from two years ago, but a bit stronger."

Chaim Chosid and his sons-in-law have to be tougher than steel to endure all this. It's enough that Eli Noah—imagine that!—he who wears a silk cap in mid-week has to be a servant to Mazepevke Jews one day a year. But he has no choice.

That's why there is one day a year when the women must be free of their daily responsibilities . . . so they can bring the holy Pesach into the house, dress up and look good in the best possible manner, and become queens at the Seder, as God has ordained.

With all the preparations for the sacred festival completed, Chaimova and her daughters changed clothes, dressed up in the finest manner, and became queens at the Seder, indeed as God has ordained. Shining and glittering in satin and silk, with pearls and diamonds, they looked so elegant one should have painted a portrait of them.

But Tsireleh's conduct was not like that of the others on this Eve of Pesach. She didn't want to dress up and primp as in years past. She looked worried, distracted, her face pale with blue rings under her eyes, like a person who could not sleep all night long and wept throughout the night.

Something had happened to our Tsireleh.

# CHAPTER 15

# This Pesach Night

We consider the beloved Uncle Pesach sweet and dear for lots of reasons.

It is sweet and dear because it reminds us that long, long ago we were liberated from the Exile of Egypt. Pesach is also sweet and dear because it comes just at the time when the entire world itself awakens, liberated, renewed, and revivified. The earth catches its breath and the sky speaks, sounding out thunder and lightning.

Everything is born afresh. Endless joy!

The holiday is also sweet and dear because poor and dejected Jews toil hard, alas, and struggle, and just barely, in the nick of time, amid great trouble, angst, and tribulations, bring in the holy holiday. Now, finally, they can rest and relax for eight days in a row.

And when I recall the name of the beloved and sweet Uncle Pesach, my happy childhood, the sweet world of my youth, rises up from the grave and sends me greetings from those precious years that will never ever return.

But if Pesach is a holiday, then the first night of Pesach is a double festival, a holiday's holiday.

Everything was quiet in Mazepevke on that Pesach night; all was tranquil and festive. Chaim Chosid concluded the Seder. He had eaten the knaidlakh, accompanied by good wine, and by the time he had sung the long final song of the Haggadah, the "Chad Gadya," he felt full as a drum.

While still at the table, Chaim Chosid felt he was dozing off. He had just rushed through the Song of Songs chanted after the Seder—God alone knows if he had managed to finish it—for entire sections swam away from him right before his eyes, just like part of a journey seems to vanish, made shorter when one is lost in thought.

So Chaim Chosid quietly slipped away from the table, undressed—and what about the bedtime "Sh'ma," the Hear O Israel prayer? What Sh'ma? Where Sh'ma?—sank into bed, and fell asleep at once.

And all the sons-in-law, who at first competed with one another to show off their refined taste in wine drinking, slowly became so drunk that when they rose from the table, they could barely stand on their feet.

Eli Noah was drunk as Lot, so soused he wouldn't even have noticed had they tied him up and thrown him outside.

True, when he stood up, he pretended to sing something from the Haggadah, stretching out a refrain from the song, "It Happened in the Middle of the Night." But his slurred words made him sound so ridiculous and his face look so foolish, his wife had to take him by one finger and lead him away, like a calf, forgive the comparison, is taken to its mama.

"Come on already. Off to bed . . . You got yourself all boozed up and you're still singing away."

And that is how on this Pesach night after the Seder at Chaim Chosid's house each person crept off to his room. Soon, snoring and whistling from many throats and noses, in various tones, resounded throughout the house.

But Tsireleh was the only one who was not asleep.

On that Pesach night Tsireleh bade farewell to her father's house. She got out of bed and, wearing a shawl on her head, a dress, and a pair of shoes, Tsireleh quietly slipped out the door.

Waiting for her there was a tall, handsome man.

Maxim Tchubinski.

It was a warm, dark night. Stars were hidden behind murky clouds. They did not want to witness a Jewish girl abandoning her father's house on such a holy night. A soft drizzle was falling, warm tears trickling from the sky, weeping for the tragedy that had befallen Chaim Chosid and his family. Still completely oblivious to what had happened, they slept the sweet sleep of happy, sincerely pious Jews on that holy festival, the most joyous of all the holidays.

Had someone woken up during that night and merely looked at Tsireleh, she would have turned back. But no one woke up. Everyone was fast asleep, in deep sweet holiday slumber.

Tsireleh, however, was shivering like a lamb, and so Maxim Tchubinski calmed her with sweet golden words.

"I love you so much," he said as he hugged her. "I'm so happy you listened and did what I asked you to do. And soon we're going to be so happy together."

Tsireleh burst into tears out of abundant happiness but also out of fright at what she had done, trusting Maxim completely and placing herself totally in his hands.

And then he brought her to the monastery.

# CHAPTER 16

# Monastery Bells Are Ringing

When Tsireleh entered the monastery, she wished that what had to happen should happen quickly, for fear that, God forbid, she might be assailed by regrets. However, she pulled herself together and swore she would be strong as steel and not let anyone persuade her to reverse course, nor let any member of her family come near her. She would just close her eyes and not see, and cover her ears and not hear.

And that's exactly what happened.

The following morning, Tsireleh heard a tumult outside. Something was going on. She sensed someone was approaching, trying to reach her. She locked herself into her little alcove and didn't move. She heard a familiar voice. She could have sworn it was her mother, weeping and wailing. So she blocked her ears not to hear, even though she felt she was being pulled by iron tongs and driven by rods. But she was keeping her word. She had succeeded.

Done.

No turning back.

Tsireleh sat all alone in her little alcove, looking out the window and listening to what was happening outside. The sun was setting, descending behind the monastery, gilding the tips of the cloisters' spires. Evening was approaching stealthily, with silent green steps;

evening was covering everything with its outspread dark wings. Evening nestled into one's soul with a strange sadness that prompted melancholy in one's heart.

The monastery bells were ringing. The monks hurrying to vespers.

"Bom, bam, bom."

That was the great bell giving forth its sounds—and every clang struck at Tsireleh's heart.

And all the other bells responded in varying tones.

"Ding, dong, ding . . . Dong, ding, dong."

And it seemed to her that the bells were not ringing but speaking, telling her what was happening at home: "ding, dong, ding," her father crying, "dong, ding, dong," her mother wailing, "dong, dong, dong," all the children weeping.

Now Tsireleh recalled her home, saw before her eyes every member of her family, each one's face with its own traits, and she felt a wave of melancholy in her heart. And she asked God—it made no difference which God—that what had to happen should happen quickly.

A constant stream of people, each time a different person, kept coming to her, preparing her to be ready. Then Maxim Tchubinski came with his golden words, telling her again and again how happy he was that she had listened to him and how happy they would soon be, and she pressed close to him, crying, weeping out of great joy and fear at what she was doing, and she prayed to God that what had to happen should happen quickly.

# CHAPTER 17

# A Dangerous Leap

Tsireleh was overjoyed that God had sent her another person—
even though it was someone like Moshkeleh Ganev—with whom
she could talk a bit, and she told him everything, omitting nothing.
Moshke listened attentively. He let her speak on and on, continue
her narrative down to its minutest details.

Neither Tsireleh nor Moshke noticed how deep into the garden
they had strolled. When Tsireleh looked about and saw how far
they had gone, she seemed startled and said:

"Let's go back."

But Moshke suddenly seized her hand with the force of iron
tongs and said:

"Stay put. You're not goin back. I've listened to everything you
told me. And now *you're* gonna have to listen to what *I'm* gonna
tell *you*."

Tsireleh stood stock still, like a plank in a wall. She looked with
fear into Moshke's eyes, unable to remove her hand from his iron
grip.

Then Moshke told her what he had to say, crisply and simply:

"I've loved you way before you ever met Maxim Tchubinski,
but I never had the guts to utter your holy name or even think
about you in my dreams, because who am I and who are you?

I'm Moshkeleh Ganev and you, you're Chaim Chosid's daughter. Some comparison!

"And now I've got a plan I must carry out, and God should strike me dead here and now if I don't carry it out.

"It's a simple plan. I pick you up and we both jump over this wall and you get on the horse with me, he's all prepared and has been waiting for me since early this morning, and we run to the nearest town and we get married. And I swear to you by God, by the God in heaven above, that I'm always gonna be your slave. For you I'll go through fire and water and you're gonna be much more happy with me than with Maxim Tchubinski because, I, Moshkeleh Ganev, love you more than forty thousand Maxim Tchubinskis can ever love you."

Without giving Tsireleh any time to think this over, Moshke picked her up like a child and climbed up on the monastery wall with her.

"Now listen," he said. "If you make even the slightest peep, I'm gonna choke you with these here hands and then throw myself off of this wall and smash my head to smithereens."

All this happened so suddenly that not only couldn't Tsireleh scream, she couldn't even catch her breath. She was like one dead, yet still shaking as if with high fever.

And when Moshke took her into his arms, about to jump off the high wall into the thorn bushes below, Tsireleh threw her small arms around Moshke's thick neck, like a child looking down into the water as it clings to a grownup standing in a pond.

Tsireleh's eyes were closed and she felt she was about to faint.

CHAPTER 18

# A Posted Letter and Some Comments by the Author

A few days later Chaim Chosid got a letter in the mail containing the following lines:

> Dear Father and beloved Mother,
> I am writing to let you know that, thank God, I am fine and well and I have remained a faithful Jewish daughter.
> I have gotten married to Moshke, who back home was called Moshkeleh Ganev.
> And I am happy, maybe even happier than all my sisters.
> And don't ask me how this all happened. It was probably something fated by God, like Reb Sholom the matchmaker says, "A match made in heaven."
> And I want to let you know, dear father and mother, that we will never come back to Mazepevke. We don't want to witness your humiliation and grief.
> May you live to be one hundred and twenty.
> I remain, from far away, your devoted daughter, who kisses you a thousand times and wishes you good health, success, and all good things.
> Give my friendly greetings to everyone.

My husband, Moshke, sends his friendly greetings to everyone.

*Your daughter,*
Tsirl

It's customary for almost all writers the world over to proclaim at the very outset of their story, even in the prologue, that they swear to their readers on a stack of Bibles—and they do this with such sincerity you'd even believe a scoundrel—that everything they write is absolutely true and not one word was dreamt up, God forbid.

Not even one.

But these writers don't realize that the more they swear, the less they will be believed.

I once had a childhood friend named Tankhel, who was a first-class liar. All the boys in school were aware of this—and Tankhel himself knew that we knew he was a liar.

So what did he do? When he had to tell us something, the first thing he did was pile on the oaths:

"Listen, fellas. I swear to God! I should drop dead here on the spot, choke on the first bite, die a strange death, turn into a stone, a bone, if what I'm tellin' you now is even the teeny-tiniest bit of a lie . . ."

And only then would he start narrating his story, which would turn out to be a top-notch whopping lie.

Based on this, I don't want to justify myself, my dear reader, and prove to you, while looking you straight in the eye, that the story I'm now narrating actually happened, precisely the way I've depicted it in this novel.

I'm just telling you it's so, and now the choice is up to you. Either take my word or don't.

But I can give you a piece of advice: take a trip to Mazepevke, stop any Jew in the middle of a street, and ask him the following question:

"Tell me, uncle, wasn't there a chap here in your town called Moshkeleh Ganev?"

This man will answer:

"What's that? Moshkeleh Ganev? The one who ran off with Chaim Chosid's daughter? What's up? Why're you asking? Any special reason?"

Then of course your reply will be:

"Nothing special. Just asking."

At this point you'll probably want to leave, but that man won't let you go. He'll start asking *you* questions:

"What do you mean, 'Nothing special. Just asking'? Since when does a Jew ask about something just like that? If you're asking, you probably know something."

And don't think you'll get rid of this chap so easily. This man you've spoken to now stops two other Jews and, while pointing a finger at you, tells them:

"Listen to this. Here I am, strolling along, and this guy comes up to me and starts asking me about Moshkeleh Ganev. So I ask him, 'Why're you asking about Moshkeleh Ganev? Any special reason?' So he answers, 'Nothing special. Just asking.'"

By now, three or four more Mazepevke Jews have joined the three standing there and now you're surrounded by all of them and they begin working on you in a different manner. One man tells the next who you are. This one says you've just seen Moshkeleh Ganev somewhere. Another says that you've just come into town with him. A third whispers into the ear of his neighbor that *you're* Moshkeleh Ganev himself.

And you thank God you've managed to tear yourself away from

them, and I'm afraid you'll also warn your grandchildren not to go to Mazepevke and never ask anyone about Moshkeleh Ganev.

So better take my word that there was indeed a Moshkeleh Ganev in Mazepevke, a Tsireleh, and a Chaim Chosid who had a beautiful wife and good-looking daughters and several sons-in-law, and all the other people included in my novel.

Ah, what has become of all of them? We might as well ask, "What's become of all of your acquaintances from long ago?" Some have died; some have moved to other places or run away, like mice in years of famine.

Chaim Chosid's wine cellar has long been closed, and the Mazepevke worthies now get together not in a tavern but in the club, where they play cards and drink pure 40 proof straight whiskey, brandy, or kvass. Not Vermouth. That's over and done with. Goodbye, Vermouth.

Chaim Chosid himself has been a resident of the True World, and Chaimova is now an old lady who wears a marriage wig, and even though her face is very wrinkled and she walks with a stoop, you can still see, today, that she had once been a beautiful woman.

Her daughters and sons-in-law have sailed, one by one, to America, where they make a living. Some people say that Eli Noah exchanged his silken cap long ago for a regular hat. Now that he's become a hundred percent Yankee, he's called "Mister," reads a newspaper, and is considered an "allrightnik."

I myself have seen a photo of him which he sent to a friend that absolutely amazed and astounded me. If someone hadn't told me that was Eli Noah, Chaim Chosid's son-in-law, I'd have thought it was a circus horseback rider, a hotel doorman, or, at the very least, a waiter at a fancy wedding.

All year long Eli Noah swats mattresses till they're clean, but comes a rich man's wedding, he shaves his chin, waxes his mustache, and puts on a white bow tie, paper shirt front, and double-breasted waistcoat with wide cuffs from which his big red hands and black nails protrude.

How about that for a free country?

Now only one matter remains: what's doing with Moshkeleh Ganev and his wife, Tsireleh.

In that case, we must ask everyone: please read on.

# CHAPTER 19

# Henekh the Cantor Looks for a Job

Several years have now passed from the time this story was written. We are now into the doleful, plaintive days of the month of Elul, just before Rosh Hashana, when Jewish children are free from school, grown-up men learn how to blow a shofar, cantors go around looking for High Holiday positions, and teachers search for jobs starting in the fall.

Meanwhile, the sky is bedecked with heavy, leaden clouds, bemoaning and shedding cold tears over the bygone summer.

During one of these Elul days, Henekh the slaughterer, or Henekh the cantor—he was both—was on his way from Sekuran to Britshan, in search of a cantorial position for Rosh Hashana and Yom Kippur.

Henekh was, as they say, a world cantor. Not that he had a worldwide reputation; rather, he was the sort of world cantor who travels about the world looking for a job. Sometimes he finds one, sometimes not. And when these cantors get a job, they lead either the holiday Morning Service or the Additional Service, or both, depending on the arrangements.

Our Henekh never charged exorbitant fees. He had never charged more than one hundred rubles, including the anticipated donations given by the congregants.

And yet, a story circulated among the Mazepevke Jews (Mazepevke has a story about everyone) about that one Sabbath when Henekh had come to a shtetl for a Rosh Hashana tryout. His singing pleased his listeners immensely, for he had a beautiful voice and precise enunciation. But when it came to negotiating his fee and Henekh found out that, exclusive of donations, they were offering him only seventy rubles, he said:

"In that case, go find yourself another cantor."

At which he snatched his walking stick and ran off.

But since all this pertains to Henekh and has nothing to do with our novel, let's return to the story at hand.

On his way from Sekuran to Britshan, Henekh was riding on a coach, not alone, of course, but in the company of other men and women. And because it was rather chilly and Henekh's clothes were frayed in spots and tattered in others, in order to protect his voice box from catching cold, God forbid, he wrapped a big, warm shawl around his head and throat.

At first the passengers' conversations consisted of the usual questions:

"What's your name?"

"Where you from?"

"Where you heading?"

But once they had their fill of talking and sighing over problems of meager livelihood and the sad fate of Jews who continually longed for the traditional blessing of "good news, salvations, and consolations," they all suddenly fell silent.

Now everyone was deeply immersed in his own affairs and concerns.

Henekh too was lost in thought, and he had plenty to ponder about, for, if God forbid—may it not happen!—he missed out on a position in Britshan, he would have absolutely no job for the coming High Holidays.

Suddenly, just as this notion was crossing his mind, in the middle of the road between Sekuran and Britshan, he saw a group of men marching in a prisoners' transport convoy, chained in pairs, their irons rattling. Behind them was a huge wagon filled with women and children.

Henekh, now deep into his thoughts, would surely have paid as much attention to this convoy as to the snows of yesteryear. They were just a bunch of crooks and lowlifes, the devil take em.

But Henekh himself didn't know what had come over him, for among the prisoners he spotted a swarthy man with dark hair and a black beard. He could have sworn this man was a Jew, and, besides, not only did he look familiar—he looked very familiar. Yet no matter how hard Henekh racked his brain and rubbed his forehead, for the life of him he could not recall who this man was.

And since Henekh had become so absorbed with this familiar-looking man, the next thing he did was scrutinize the wagon carrying the women and children. There he noticed a beautiful woman wearing a red kerchief on her head, holding a child in her arms. Henekh could have sworn this was a Jewish woman, one who looked familiar—in fact, very familiar indeed.

"What amazing things can suddenly happen," Henekh said to himself, as his fingers played with his bottle-like sidecurls and he wrapped the shawl tighter around his neck.

Suddenly, he heard someone calling him by name:

"Reb Henekh! Reb Henekh!"

# CHAPTER 20

# What a Story! What a Tale!

Henekh turned to look. Calling to him was the beautiful young woman with the red kerchief holding a child in her arms. Startled, Henekh felt he'd become a pillar of salt.

Who can that be? he wondered.

"Reb Henekh? Don't you recognize me? I'm Tsireleh, Chaim Chosid's daughter, Chaim Chosid's youngest daughter. Once you're back home in Mazepevke, please send my warm greetings to my father and mother and everyone in the family. And please be sure to tell them that we are on our way to Irkutsk, in Siberia. Please, please don't forget to send warm greetings to my father."

Tsireleh added something and gestured with her hands, but because the wagons were now moving further apart, Henekh could no longer hear what she was saying. He only heard some of the prisoners laughing together and singing a strange little rhymed ditty whose meaning was difficult to understand:

Hey, Yenkel, Sarah sweet.
Gimme brandy, gimme meat.

Evidently, everyone in the crowd liked this ditty. But what pleased them most was the clowning of one of their fellow prisoners, a tall chap with a red, pockmarked face. In order to irritate the Jews, he had taken the edge of his greatcoat to his lips, imitating how a

Jew kisses his ritual fringes, and, while looking at Henekh rocked his head back and forth many times, as though fervently praying.

But Henekh disregarded him like Haman the Purim noisemakers when the Scroll of Esther is chanted. Henekh was busy with another matter. This meeting shook him to the core.

He then put two and two together and concluded that no doubt the swarthy man with the black beard was surely none other than Tsireleh's husband, Moshkeleh Ganev. And Henekh could not stop wondering about this, and saying softly to himself:

"What a story! What a tale! The amazing things that can happen in this world."

This story had naturally aroused the curiosity of Henekh's fellow passengers on the coach.

"Who's that young woman who just asked you to send greetings to her family? Let's hear some more about this story. . . ."

But no matter how much they pestered him they were unable to get one solitary word out of him.

Henekh the cantor could not stop gesticulating; he grew more and more excited, and repeated again and again, "What a story! What a tale! The amazing things that can happen in this world!"

"Then tell it to us too. We also want to hear this amazing story."

"It's the sort of story, you hear, that can only happen once in a hundred years. What a story! What a tale! The unbelievable things that can happen in this world!"

And Henekh was unable to say another word. He didn't know where to begin. With Tsireleh or with Moshkeleh Ganev? With events that occurred later on or with those that took place at the beginning?

A bitter smile was frozen on Henekh's face as his memories took him and brought him far away, to where he himself did not know—somewhere behind the legendary Hills of Darkness.

Now a wind came and light rain began to fall. The coachman whistled and jabbered away and the horses moved apace with neat little steps. The wagon wheels rolled along on the wet ground, the coach shook, and all the passengers swayed and bounced and bumped shoulders and, at times, foreheads.

Henekh, too, wrapped in his warm shawl, swayed back and forth, and his windblown, bottle-like sidecurls, bobbing as if on little springs, gave him much added charm.

# Other Books by Curt Leviant

## NOVELS

*The Yemenite Girl*

*The Man Who Thought He Was Messiah*

*Partita in Venice*

*Diary of an Adulterous Woman*

*Ladies and Gentlemen, the Original Music of the Hebrew Alphabet and Weekend in Mustara* (two novellas)

*A Novel of Klass*

*King of Yiddish*

*Zix Zexy Ztories*

*Kafka's Son*

*Katz or Cats—Or, How Jesus Became My Rival in Love*

*Me, Mo, Mu, Ma & Mod (Or, Which Will It Be, Me and Mazal or Gila and Me?)*

## TRANSLATIONS FROM YIDDISH
## WITH INTRODUCTIONS

*Old Country Tales*, by Sholom Aleichem

*Some Laughter, Some Tales*, by Sholom Aleichem

*From the Fair, the Autobiography of Sholom Aleichem*

*The Song of Songs*, by Sholom Aleichem

*Happy New Year and Other Stories*, by Sholom Aleichem

*My First Love Affair and Other Stories*, by Sholom Aleichem

*The Agunah*, by Chaim Grade

*The Yeshiva*, by Chaim Grade

*The Yeshiva*, vol. II, *Masters and Disciples*, by Chaim Grade
*The Seven Little Lanes*, by Chaim Grade
*The Jewish Government and Other Stories*, by Lamed Shapiro
*The Heart-Stirring Sermon and Other Stories*, by Avraham Reisen
*More Stories from My Father's Court*, by Isaac Bashevis Singer
*The Jewish Book of Fables*, by Eliezer Shtaynbarg

TRANSLATED AND EDITED TEXTS FROM
HEBREW WITH INTRODUCTIONS

*King Artus, a Hebrew Arthurian Romance of 1279*
*Masterpieces of Hebrew Literature: A Treasury of 2000 Years of
Jewish Creativity*
*The Golem and the Wondrous Deeds of the Maharal of Prague*, by
Yudl Rosenberg

# About the Translator

Curt Leviant is the prize-winning author or translator of more than twenty-five books. Besides Sholom Aleichem, other Yiddish writers he has translated include Chaim Grade, Isaac Bashevis Singer, and Avraham Reisen.

Curt Leviant's novels have been translated into Hebrew and ten European languages. Among them are *The Yemenite Girl*; *Kafka's Son*, hailed in France as "a work of genius"; and the international best seller *Diary of an Adulterous Woman*. For the latter novel, critics compared Leviant to Flaubert, Tolstoy, Milan Kundera, Nabokov, and Vargas Llosa.

Curt Leviant has won the Wallant Award for his fiction and several national and international literary fellowships, including those given by the National Endowment for the Humanities, the National Endowment for the Arts, and the New Jersey Council on the Arts. He has also been awarded creative writing residences from the Rockefeller Foundation at Bellagio, the Jerusalem Foundation, and the Venice-based Emily Harvey Foundation. He is also the editor of *Masterpieces of Hebrew Literature: A Treasury of 2000 Years of Jewish Creativity*, published by The Jewish Publication Society.